How to Analyze the Works of

STEPHEN
KING

by Marcia Amidon Lusted

ABDO
Publishing Company

Essential Critiques

How to Analyze the Works of
STEPHEN
KING

by Marcia Amidon Lusted

Content Consultant: Benjamin J. Robertson, instructor,
Department of English, University of Colorado at Boulder

Credits

Published by ABDO Publishing Company, 8000 West 78th Street, Edina, Minnesota 55439. Copyright © 2011 by Abdo Consulting Group, Inc. International copyrights reserved in all countries. No part of this book may be reproduced in any form without written permission from the publisher. The Essential Library™ is a trademark and logo of ABDO Publishing Company.

Printed in the United States of America, North Mankato, Minnesota
062010
092010

Editor: Holly Saari
Copy Editor: Paula Lewis
Interior Design and Production: Marie Tupy
Cover Design: Marie Tupy

Library of Congress Cataloging-in-Publication Data
Lüsted, Marcia Amidon.
  How to analyze the works of Stephen King / Marcia Amidon Lusted.
    p. cm. — (Essential critiques)
  Includes bibliographical references.
  ISBN 978-1-61613-536-2
  1. King, Stephen, 1947—Criticism and interpretation—Juvenile literature. 2. Horror tales, American—History and criticism—Juvenile literature. I. Title.
  PS3561.I483Z753 2010
  813'.54—dc22
                                        2010015007

Table of Contents

Chapter

1

Introduction to Critiques

What Is Critical Theory?

What do you usually do when you read a book? You probably absorb the specific language style of the book. You learn about the characters as they are developed through thoughts, dialogue, and other interactions. You may like or dislike a character more than others. You might be drawn in by the plot of the book, eager to find out what happens at the end. Yet these are only a few of many possible ways of understanding and appreciating a book. What if you are interested in delving more deeply? You might want to learn more about the author and how his or her personal background is reflected in the book. Or you might want to examine what the book says about society—how it depicts the roles of

The end.

women and minorities, for example. If so, you have entered the realm of critical theory.

Critical theory helps you learn how various works of art, literature, music, theater, film, and other endeavors either support or challenge the way society behaves. Critical theory is the evaluation and interpretation of a work using different philosophies, or schools of thought. Critical theory can be used to understand all types of cultural productions.

There are many different critical theories. If you are analyzing literature, each theory asks you to look at the work from a different perspective. Some theories address social issues, while others focus on the writer's life or the time period in which the book was written or set. For example, the critical theory that asks how an author's life affected the work is called biographical criticism. Other common schools of criticism include historical criticism, feminist criticism, psychological criticism, and New Criticism, which examines a work solely within the context of the work itself.

What Is the Purpose of Critical Theory?

Critical theory can open your mind to new ways of thinking. It can help you evaluate a book from a new perspective, directing your attention to issues and messages you may not otherwise recognize in a work. For example, applying feminist criticism to a book may make you aware of female stereotypes perpetuated in the work. Applying a critical theory to a book helps you learn about the person who created it or the society that enjoyed it. You can also explore how the work is perceived by current cultures.

How Do You Apply Critical Theory?

You conduct a critique when you use a critical theory to examine and question a work. The theory you choose is a lens through which you can view the work, or a springboard for asking questions about the work. Applying a critical theory helps you think critically about the work. You are free to question the work and make an assertion about it. If you choose to examine a book using biographical theory, for example, you want to know how the author's personal background or education inspired or shaped the work. You could explore why the author was drawn to the story. For instance, are there any parallels between a particular character's life and the author's life?

Forming a Thesis

Ask your question and find answers in the work or other related materials. Then you can create a thesis. The thesis is the key point in your critique. It is your argument about the work based on the tenets, or beliefs, of the theory you are using. For example, if you are using biographical theory to ask how the author's life inspired the work, your thesis could be worded as follows: Writer Teng Xiong, raised in refugee camps in

> **How to Make a Thesis Statement**
>
> In a critique, a thesis statement typically appears at the end of the introductory paragraph. It is usually only one sentence long and states the author's main idea.

southeast Asia, drew upon her experiences to write the novel *No Home for Me.*

Providing Evidence

Once you have formed a thesis, you must provide evidence to support it. Evidence might take the form of examples and quotations from the work itself—such as dialogue from a character. Articles about the book or personal interviews with the author might also support your ideas. You may wish to address what other critics have written about the work. Quotes from these individuals may help support your claim. If you find any quotes or examples that contradict your thesis, you will need to create an argument against them. For instance: Many critics have pointed to the protagonist of *No Home for Me* as a powerless victim of circumstances. However, in the chapter "My Destiny," she is clearly depicted as someone who seeks to shape her own future.

How to Support a Thesis Statement

A critique should include several arguments. Arguments support a thesis claim. An argument is one or two sentences long and is supported by evidence from the work being discussed.

Organize the arguments into paragraphs. These paragraphs make up the body of the critique.

In This Book

In this book, you will read summaries of famous books by writer Stephen King, each followed by a critique. Each critique will use one theory and apply it to one work. Critical thinking sections will give you a chance to consider other theses and questions about the work. Did you agree with the author's application of the theory? What other questions are raised by the thesis and its arguments? You can also find out what other critics think about each particular book. Then, in the You Critique It section in the final pages of this book, you will have an opportunity to create your own critique.

Look for the Guides

Throughout the chapters that analyze the works, thesis statements have been highlighted. The box next to the thesis helps explain what questions are being raised about the work. Supporting arguments have been underlined. The boxes next to the arguments help explain how these points support the thesis. Look for these guides throughout each critique.

Essential Critiques

Stephen King is one of the most prolific American writers.

2

A Closer Look at Stephen King

Stephen King, one of the most popular writers in the United States, was born in Portland, Maine, on September 21, 1947. He was the second son of Donald and Nellie King. His father abandoned the family when Stephen was two, leaving Stephen and his older brother, David, to be raised by their mother. After Donald left, the family moved to Indiana and Connecticut before returning to Durham, Maine. Nellie worked many different jobs to support her family; while they did not have a lot of money, they never went hungry.

Introduction to Horror

When Stephen was around 13 years old, he had his first exposure to quality horror fiction. While exploring a relative's attic, he found a box filled with his father's belongings, including a copy of an H. P. Lovecraft anthology of horror stories. King has also noted that the Ripley's Believe It or Not! series of paperback books introduced him to amazing and unusual facts.

Published Author

Stephen was in high school when his first short story, "I Was a Teenage Grave Robber," was published in 1965 in the *Comics Review*. During his time at the University of Maine at Orono, he wrote several novels that were later published under the pseudonym Richard Bachman. In 1970, Stephen graduated with a degree in English and teaching credentials. However, he was unable to find a teaching job. Instead, he worked odd jobs while continuing to sell short stories to magazines. In 1971, he married Tabitha Spruce and began teaching high school English at Hampden Academy in Hampden, Maine. He continued to write in the evening and on weekends. In 1973, he sold his first novel, *Carrie*, which enabled him to write full-time.

Stephen and Tabitha moved several times before settling down permanently in Maine. Stephen continued to write successful books. In 1978, he began teaching creative writing at the University of Maine. During the 1980s, Stephen became addicted to drugs and alcohol. After an intervention by his family, he was able to quit.

Near-Fatal Accident

In 1999, King was walking along the shoulder of a highway in Center Lovell, Maine, where he lived. Suddenly, a car struck him. He suffered a collapsed right lung, multiple fractures in his right leg, cuts to his scalp, and a broken hip. He was hospitalized for three weeks. King underwent five operations and physical therapy, but he was unable to write for any length of time because of the pain. In 2002, King announced he would stop writing, partly because of his frustration with his injuries. Since that announcement, however, King has continued to write and has even published several novels.

Acclaim and Popularity

In 2003, King received the National Book Foundation Medal for Distinguished Contribution to American Letters. Controversy arose because the medal was awarded to a writer of popular fiction rather than a more literary writer. However, Neil Baldwin, executive director of the National Book Foundation, said in his announcement:

> Stephen King's writing is securely rooted in the great American tradition that glorifies spirit-of-place and the abiding power of narrative. He crafts stylish, mind-bending page-turners that contain profound moral truths—some beautiful, some harrowing— about our inner lives. This award commemorates Mr. King's well-earned place of distinction in the wide world of readers and booklovers of all ages.[1]

King writes more than novels. He has written stories exclusively for the Internet and for e-book readers. And in October 2009, it was announced that he would help write a new comic book series called American Vampire.

Many of King's stories have been made into movies as well. King has had cameo roles in several of them. He also directed the movie *Maximum Overdrive*, which is an adaptation of his short story "Trucks."

King divides his time between Bangor, Maine, and Florida. An active philanthropist, he helps raise money for many different causes and provides scholarships for Maine high school students. He and his wife, Tabitha, also own a radio station group in Maine.

King continues to be one of the best-selling novelists in the world and the most financially successful horror writer in history. Because of the wide-ranging popularity of his books and movie adaptations, he is considered an American icon.

King received the Lifetime Achievement Award from the Canadian Booksellers Association in 2007.

IF YOU'VE GOT
A TASTE FOR TERROR...
TAKE CARRIE TO THE PROM.

"CARRIE"

If only they knew she had the power.

A PAUL MONASH Production A BRIAN DePALMA Film "CARRIE"
starring SISSY SPACEK
JOHN TRAVOLTA and PIPER LAURIE · Screenplay by LAWRENCE D. COHEN
Based on the novel by STEPHEN KING · Produced by PAUL MONASH · Directed by BRIAN DePALMA
Production Services by Carrie's Group

RESTRICTED

United Artists

King's *Carrie* was made into a movie, which was released in 1976.

3

Summary of *Carrie*

King's first book, *Carrie*, was published in 1974. King had previously published magazine fiction, but *Carrie* was his first full-length published novel. The book's style is a departure from straightforward fictional narrative. While it includes narrative, it also includes fictional news reports, interviews, and transcripts of legal proceedings. These nontraditional elements make the story seem real.

Taunting and Telekinesis

Carrie tells the story of Carrie White, a 16-year-old outcast. Overweight and unattractive, she lives with her fanatically religious mother, who does not let her dress and act like other girls her age. Carrie's peers constantly ridicule her.

As the story opens, Carrie is showering in the locker room after her high school gym class. Suddenly, she experiences the onset of her first menstrual period. The event is traumatic for her because she does not know what is happening. The other girls in the locker room begin to yell and throw feminine hygiene products at her. Even her gym teacher displays impatience and disgust with Carrie.

Carrie's mother, Margaret White, believes that Carrie's period is a sign that Carrie has sinned. She forces Carrie into a closet for hours to pray and repent—an abusive punishment frequently imposed upon Carrie. During this instance, however, Carrie rediscovers her talent of telekinesis—she can move objects with just her mind. She used this power several times as a child. However, her mother's negative reaction and abuse had caused Carrie to suppress the memories. Now, the onset of menstruation has unlocked them.

Revenge

Meanwhile, two of the girls from the scene in the locker room, Sue Snell and Chris Hargensen, have different reactions to what happened there.

Sue feels guilty about taunting Carrie. In contrast, Chris's hatred for Carrie increases when she learns that the entire class will be punished with a week's detention as a result of the locker-room incident. Chris skips the detention, only to find out that she cannot attend her senior prom as a consequence. She wants to make a protest, but her lawyer father will not intervene on her behalf. Chris, with the help of her boyfriend, Billy Nolan, vows to get revenge on Carrie.

Margaret White often punishes and represses Carrie.

Carrie begins to experiment with her newly rediscovered ability. She strengthens it by performing mental exercises, such as lifting increasingly heavy objects using only her mind. At the same time, Sue Snell's lingering feeling of guilt leads her to ask her boyfriend, Tommy Ross, to take Carrie to the prom instead of her. Tommy agrees and asks Carrie, who reluctantly accepts.

The Prom

After accepting Tommy's offer, Carrie undergoes a physical transformation. She buys fabric to sew her prom dress and makes other improvements to her appearance. But when Carrie tells her mother about the upcoming dance, Margaret White orders Carrie to go to the closet to pray and repent. Carrie refuses and tells her mother that from now on, circumstances will be changing in their lives.

Chris Hargensen learns that Carrie will be going to the prom with Tommy Ross. She comes up with a plan to hang buckets of pig blood from the ceiling above the prom king's and queen's thrones. She sends Billy to a nearby farm, where he and his friends kill several pigs and collect their blood. Chris convinces classmates to vote for Carrie and Tommy as queen and king.

While Carrie is getting dressed on the night of the prom, her mother tries to convince her that she is sinning. Finally, Carrie uses her now-strong telekinesis to make her mother leave the room. Tommy takes Carrie to the prom, where they mingle with his friends. Carrie begins to feel liked and accepted, and Tommy has begun to fall in love with her. He casts the tie vote for them to be the royal couple, believing that Carrie deserves to experience the ultimate prom night.

Tragic Ending

Tommy and Carrie are voted king and queen. As they climb the stairs to the stage, Chris Hargensen pulls the string that dumps pig blood all over Carrie. The bucket hits Tommy in the head, knocking him unconscious. As the silent gymnasium erupts into nervous laughter, Carrie understands that she has been tricked and is the target of yet another joke. In her anger, she takes full advantage of her renewed mental powers. She locks the gym doors and takes actions that result in a massive fire. As Carrie leaves the gym and heads into the town, most of the

As Carrie is crowned prom queen, a bucket of pig blood is dumped on her.

students and teachers at the prom are trapped and killed in the fire, including Tommy Ross. Chris and Billy have escaped.

Carrie walks through town, causing devastation everywhere she goes. When she finally arrives home, Carrie's mother stabs her with a butcher knife. Carrie stops her mother's heart, killing her.

Then she continues to wander through town, forcing the car in which Chris and Billy are riding to crash into a building. Carrie has one final encounter with Sue Snell, who did not attend the prom but was drawn out of her house as the fire raged. Sue sees that Carrie is dying and cradles her. Carrie looks inside Sue's mind and realizes that Sue did not mean to trick her. Then Carrie dies.

The book ends with a letter from an unknown woman in Georgia to her sister. The woman describes her young daughter's amazing ability to make things move by themselves. This last portion implies that Carrie's powers were not limited to her.

Feminist criticism analyzes how Carrie and other female characters are portrayed in the novel.

Chapter

4

How to Apply Feminist Criticism to *Carrie*

No.2

What Is Feminist Criticism?

In general, feminism is the belief that women should have the same opportunities and rights as men. Some types of feminism debate certain ideas—for example, the role of women's power over their bodies. However, most types of feminism challenge traditional roles women have held throughout history.

A feminist critique examines how female characters are portrayed, how they are treated by other characters, and the images they leave with the reader. Readers who apply feminist criticism look for stereotypes of women. Are those stereotypes undermined or reinforced? Are females underrepresented in the work? What roles do they play? How does the work handle gender inequality?

Critique

Published in 1974, *Carrie* was written during the rise of the feminist movement. During this time, an increasing number of women began to question their roles and purpose in society. They began to explore their power and were no longer willing to be confined to their homes as housewives. In King's *Carrie*, the protagonist, Carrie, symbolizes the development of the feminist movement—she transforms from a stereotypical female victim to a complex, powerful woman.

At the beginning of the novel, Carrie is controlled by her mother, who represents the masculine authority of the Christian church. Throughout history, the church has been almost entirely run by men— male priests, bishops, and popes.

Thesis Statement

The thesis statement in this critique is: "In King's *Carrie*, the protagonist, Carrie, symbolizes the development of the feminist movement— she transforms from a stereotypical female victim to a complex, powerful woman." This thesis addresses the question: Is Carrie a stereotypical portrayal of a woman? This thesis states she is at first, and then later she rejects this portrayal.

Argument One

The author of this essay has begun to argue the thesis. Her first point states: "At the beginning of the novel, Carrie is controlled by her mother, who represents the masculine authority of the Christian church." This point addresses the first part of the thesis and shows how Carrie is a victim of male power at the start of the novel. The author will back up this point in the following paragraphs.

These male authorities have controlled women's actions, clothing, and their roles in the home and society. In the past, women were instructed to dress and act modestly and to avoid wearing cosmetics. Their focus was to be on their husbands and households. Church authorities justified their position with biblical passages. For example, in the book of Ephesians, it states: "For wives, this means submit to your husbands as to the Lord. For a husband is the head of his wife as Christ is the head of the church. He is the Savior of his body, the church."[1]

In *Carrie*, Margaret White rules her daughter with the same restrictive beliefs about women that the Bible and the patriarchal church have espoused. Following the most traditional edicts of the Bible, Margaret makes Carrie dress in a modest fashion from long ago. Carrie wears "her blouse, her hateful knee-length skirt, her slip, her girdle, her pettipants, her garter belt, her stockings."[2]

When Carrie begins menstruating, the situation with her mother becomes even more intense. Menstruation is the process where a woman's uterus sheds its lining once a month. Once a girl starts menstruating, she is capable of bearing children.

In many cultures, menstruation is also a symbolic coming of age for a young woman, since she leaves childhood behind and can now be considered ready for marriage and childbirth. Menstruation is also a traditional symbol of femininity, since it symbolizes fertility and the ability to bear children, something that sets women apart from girls and men.

Argument Two

The second point in the essay is: "Margaret tries to instill in her daughter the misogynistic belief that the natural process of menstruation symbolizes the biblical curse of Eve." This point addresses one belief about menstruation that oppresses women, just like the masculine church.

Margaret tries to instill in her daughter the misogynistic belief that the natural process of menstruation symbolizes the biblical curse of Eve. According to the Bible, God gave Eve the punishment of a more painful childbirth after she ate the forbidden fruit. Margaret punishes Carrie for the onset of menstruation, which signals Carrie's ability to experience the curse of a painful childbirth. Margaret forces her daughter to pray and repent for something Carrie has no control over. Margaret says, "Get up, woman. Let's us get in and pray. Let's us pray to Jesus for our woman-weak, wicked sinning souls."[3]

Margaret may punish Carrie for menstruation, but this event ultimately empowers the teenager. Menstruation shows Carrie has become a woman capable of childbirth; it also sparks her forgotten telekinetic powers. As such, her telekinetic ability represents a uniquely feminine power. Carrie's situation mirrors that of women in the 1970s: as they realized they did have power and ability, they began to use their strengths in new ways. Carrie finds that the more she uses her powers, the stronger she gets: "She kept waiting for the power to abate, but it remained at high water with no sign of waning."[4] Like Carrie, women realized they had the potential to achieve more than they imagined.

When Carrie stands up to her mother, she is simultaneously rejecting the masculine power of the church and reclaiming her

Argument Three

The author's third point of the essay is: "Margaret may punish Carrie for menstruation, but this event ultimately empowers the teenager." This point is symbolic of the feminist movement. Women were oppressed by a masculine society but fought for their rights and became empowered.

Argument Four

The fourth point of the essay is: "When Carrie stands up to her mother, she is simultaneously rejecting the masculine power of the church and reclaiming her own feminine power." This point shows the symbolism of Carrie's rejection. She is rejecting her mother, but, more important, she is rejecting masculine influence.

own feminine power. She says, "I only want to be let to live my own life. I . . . I don't like yours."[5] Carrie insists on going to the prom against her mother's wishes. In Margaret's view, Carrie is rejecting her faith. As Carrie gets ready, Margaret enters the room. Margaret offers Carrie one more chance to return to the faith of the church. She wants Carrie to destroy the prom dress—the symbol of Carrie's newfound independence. Margaret says, "Take it off, Carrie. We'll go down and burn it in the incinerator together, and then pray for forgiveness. We'll do penance."[6]

Carrie, however, refuses to do so. She uses her telekinetic ability to physically propel her mother out of the room. By standing up to her mother, Carrie mirrors women in the 1970s. Carrie's telekinetic power can be likened to sexual power, as both are specifically linked to the female condition. During that decade, women gained their sexual power. They gained confidence to stand up to a controlling patriarchal society.

Carrie becomes a symbol of feminine power; however, she is not one-dimensional. In fact,

Argument Five

The final point of the essay is: "Carrie becomes a symbol of feminine power; however, she is not one-dimensional." Carrie has changed from a stereotypical female into a complex character.

By putting on her prom dress, Carrie rejects her mother's symbolic masculine authority.

she becomes a monster. She uses her telekinesis to kill her mother, her peers, and other townspeople in revenge for what occurs at the prom. In her mind, she faces the choice of maintaining her power by whatever means necessary or returning to her previous, dominated existence. She decides to do the former. Retaining her power requires murdering many people, including her mother.

Conclusion

This final paragraph is the conclusion of the critique. It sums up the author's arguments and partially restates the original thesis, which has now been argued and supported with evidence from the text. The conclusion also provides the reader with a new thought—Carrie joins male literary characters who are morally complex.

At the beginning of the novel, Carrie is a female victim of a masculine authority. Her transformation mirrors that of women during the 1970s feminist movement: she rejects male-imposed limitations and uses her rediscovered feminine abilities to become a more complex, powerful woman. By the novel's end, Carrie is both a hero and a villain. In this way, King anticipates the future of the feminist movement. To be a powerful woman does not require one to live a model existence. Women can break not only the boundaries of their conventional roles; they can also break the very boundaries of evil and good—as male characters have done for centuries. Carrie joins a rich tradition of complex, morally compromised male characters.

Thinking Critically about *Carrie*

Now it's your turn to assess the critique.
Consider these questions:

1. The thesis argues that Carrie's change
   throughout the novel represents the change in
   women's roles in society. Do you agree? Why or
   why not?

2. What was the most interesting argument made?
   What was the strongest one? What was the
   weakest? Were the points backed up with strong
   evidence from the book? Did the arguments
   support the thesis?

3. The goal of a conclusion is sometimes more
   than summarizing. A conclusion can also leave
   the reader with a new, related idea. Do you think
   this conclusion effectively introduces a new
   idea? What is it?

Other Approaches

The essay you read is one possible way to apply a feminist approach to a critique of *Carrie*. What are some other ways you could approach it? Analyzing a work using a feminist approach looks at how women are portrayed and treated in that work. Following are two alternate approaches. The first approach examines how the book portrays female biology as horrifying and disgusting. The second approach examines the secondary, stereotypical characters in the novel.

Fearing Female Biology

One critic of King's work, Kate Cielinski, maintains that *Carrie* shows King's disgust at the process of menstruation and "shows women themselves being horrified by their own biology."[7] She feels that King often has female monsters in his novels and that he may be preoccupied with or fear the opposite sex. "The very fact that he wrote an entire book about menstruation and the doom it brings—speaks largely of those fears."[8]

The thesis statement for analyzing the work based on how female biology is portrayed may be: *Carrie* is a direct reflection of the fear and disgust men and women feel about female biology.

Stereotypical Female Roles

Although a feminist analysis of the novel may prove Carrie is more than a simple female stereotype, exploration of other characters, such as Chris and Sue, may reveal other female stereotypes. These stereotypical characters could be further examined for meaning and the roles they play in the novel.

The thesis statement for analyzing *Carrie* based on the stereotypical female characters of Chris and Sue might be: While on the surface *Carrie* may seem to be a new kind of horror novel that portrays a complex female character, Carrie, the stereotypical characters of Chris Hargensen and Sue Snell firmly place the novel in the formulaic horror genre. This thesis addresses the question: Besides Carrie, how are the female characters portrayed in *Carrie* and what does this mean?

Paul Edgecomb didn't believe in miracles.

Until the day he met one.

THE
GREEN MILE

From the Director of "The Shawshank Redemption"

CASTLE ROCK ENTERTAINMENT Presents A DARKWOODS Production
TOM HANKS "THE GREEN MILE" DAVID MORSE BONNIE HUNT MICHAEL CLARKE DUNCAN JAMES CROMWELL MICHAEL JETER
GRAHAM GREENE DOUG HUTCHISON SAM ROCKWELL BARRY PEPPER JEFFREY DeMUNN PATRICIA CLARKSON HARRY DEAN STANTON Music by THOMAS NEWMAN
Costume Designer KARYN WAGNER Edited by RICHARD FRANCIS-BRUCE, A.C.E. Production Designer TERENCE MARSH Director of Photography DAVID TATTERSALL, B.S.C. Based upon the Novel by STEPHEN KING
Produced by DAVID VALDES and FRANK DARABONT DECEMBER 17 Written for the Screen and Directed by FRANK DARABONT

www.castle-rock.com   www.thegreenmile.com

The Green Mile was released as a film in 1999. Tom Hanks played the role of Paul Edgecomb.

5

Summary of
The Green Mile

King wrote *The Green Mile* in 1996. He originally published it as a serial novel in six installments. The complete book was then reissued in one volume.

Retelling a Story

The story is set at the Cold Mountain Penitentiary in the South; it is narrated by Paul Edgecomb. Once a superintendent at the prison, Paul now is an old man living in a nursing home. His story dates back to the year 1932, during the Great Depression. At this time, Paul was the supervisor of the cell block that housed prisoners who had been sentenced to death. The "green mile" refers to the block's long, green hallway leading to the electric chair.

One of the prisoners in Paul's cell block is Eduard Delacroix, known as Del, a white man imprisoned for arson and murder. Del befriends a mouse he names Mr. Jingles. Del teaches the mouse tricks, and the creature supposedly communicates to him by whispering. William Wharton, a white man known as Wild Bill, is a dangerous mass murderer. John Coffey, an African-American man, is accused of raping and murdering two little girls. Although Paul Edgecomb remembers several other prisoners from the cell block, the story focuses on these three.

Also inhabiting the green mile are several of Paul's co-workers, including a prison guard named Percy Wetmore. Percy takes pleasure in aggravating the prisoners. Because he is related to the governor, Paul and his fellow guards are powerless to stop Percy's abuse.

A Prisoner with Special Gifts

Soon after John Coffey is brought to the prison, Paul realizes there is something unusual about him. First, John heals Paul's urinary tract infection with just a touch of his hands. Later, he heals Mr. Jingles after Percy deliberately steps on the mouse in an attempt to kill it.

Percy has applied for a job transfer to the state's mental institution. He tells the other guards that he will leave only if he is put in charge of the next execution, as he has been permitted only to assist at previous executions. Desperate to get rid of him, Paul agrees, and Percy is allowed to set up and run Del's execution. However, instead of placing a sponge soaked in salt water inside the electrode cap that Del will wear, Percy deliberately substitutes a dry sponge instead. (Salt water conducts the electricity to the brain more quickly and kills the prisoner faster and with less pain.) Del dies a slow, torturous death—literally burning alive in the electric chair.

Paul learns that the prison superintendent's wife, Melinda Moores, is suffering from an inoperable brain tumor. As she becomes more and more ill, Melinda begins to experience episodes when she unknowingly uses extremely foul language—in complete opposition to her usual kind and loving nature. Paul, thinking of John Coffey's healing powers, risks losing his job to take John to the home of the Moores to heal Melinda.

Percy has not yet transferred from the green mile. In order to allow John to leave, the other guards force Percy into a straightjacket and place him in a padded restraint room. They take John to Melinda, where he heals her by inhaling what look like black bugs from her lungs. Such bugs had been present at John's previous episodes of healing; he had always immediately exhaled them. This time John deliberately keeps them in his body and becomes ill. John grows more and more incapacitated as the guards bring him back to the prison. There, John grabs Percy and exhales the bugs into Percy's mouth. This passes Melinda's disease onto him. Stunned, Percy draws a gun and kills Wild Bill Wharton before lapsing into a catatonic state. He is transferred to the state mental institution as a patient, not as a guard.

Executed Despite Innocence

Through his conversations with John, Paul eventually learns that John did not murder the two little girls the authorities found with him. Rather, he had come across them after Wild Bill Wharton raped and murdered them. He was trying to bring them back to life when he was found. As an African American in the 1930s, John became the victim of racism. Despite his innocence, John was convicted

of the crime; his execution would still take place. John is worn down by the cruelty of the world and his sensitivity to other people's thoughts and feelings. Paul feels that John is actually relieved when he is executed.

John Coffey is portrayed as a kind and gentle character in the movie adaption of *The Green Mile*.

The story returns to the present day. Paul is now 104 years old. As a side effect of being healed by John, his life has been extended beyond its natural span. The reader discovers that Paul is taking care of Mr. Jingles, who is also living an unnaturally long life. The book ends as Paul wonders just how much longer he will live.

John Coffey serves as the archetypal Christ figure in *The Green Mile*.

How to Apply Archetype Theory to *The Green Mile*

No.2

What Is Archetype Theory?

Archetype theory traces its roots to Carl Jung, a well-known Swiss psychologist who lived from 1875 to 1961. Jung believed that an individual's personality could be divided into three parts: the personal conscious, the personal unconscious, and the collective unconscious.

The personal conscious is the mind during a wakened state. The personal unconscious includes memories—those that are easily brought to mind as well as those that may be suppressed and not easily accessed. The collective unconscious can be thought of as a kind of "psychic inheritance." It includes a vast store of not just individual experiences but human experiences as a species. It is a kind of knowledge that is not learned—we are all born with it. While an individual cannot directly access the collective unconscious, it does influence experiences and behaviors, especially emotional ones. We can catch only glimpses of the collective unconscious through its influences on us.

According to Jung, the collective unconscious contains archetypes, or models of behavior or personalities. Jung identified certain archetypes, such as the hero or the wise old man, the maiden, the father, the mother, and the child. These archetypes share general characteristics, and they have been portrayed in similar forms again and again over the ages in literature. However, Jung said that the number of archetypes is limitless.

According to archetype theory, identifying archetypes in literature can heighten a reader's experience. For example, archetypes trigger certain emotional responses in a reader, and they can be used to explore and understand works of literature. Archetype theory helps readers organize their responses to what they are reading.

Critique

One of the archetypes that can be explored through literature is the Christ figure. This refers directly to Jesus Christ of Christianity, who came to Earth to save humankind from its sins. The archetypal Christ figure has a distinct set of attributes: the person is self-sacrificing and attracts followers. A Christ figure can perform miracles, especially healing, and spends time alone in some sort of wilderness. A Christ figure is often an unlikely hero and someone who transforms the lives of others. In *The Green Mile*, the archetypal Christ figure of John Coffey serves to heighten themes of compassion and sacrifice.

Several details in *The Green Mile* indicate that John is a Christ figure. His name is the first clue. John shares the initials J. C. with Jesus Christ. John is similar to Christ in many other ways, too. Like Christ, he spent time wandering the countryside, with no real home. In fact, John had been wandering in the woods

Thesis Statement

The thesis statement of this essay is: "In *The Green Mile*, the archetypal Christ figure of John Coffey serves to heighten themes of compassion and sacrifice." This thesis statement addresses the question: What common character type is used in the novel and why?

Argument One

The author has begun to argue her thesis. This is her first point: "Several details in *The Green Mile* indicate that John is a Christ figure." This point lays the groundwork for the thesis statement. The next few paragraphs back up this argument by comparing evidence from the book with the details of Jesus's life.

when he came upon the two murdered girls. Like Christ, John attracts people who come to believe in him. John has a profound impact on the prison guard Paul Edgecomb, who feels pulled toward John without quite knowing why. Paul remarks, "I did something I'd never done to a prisoner before then—I offered him my hand. Even now I don't know why."[1] Also like Christ, John has the ability to perform miracles of healing. He heals Paul, the mouse, and the warden's wife.

Christ bestows everlasting life upon those who believe in him. Similarly, John seems to bestow everlasting life on those he heals. Paul and Mr. Jingles have unusually extended life spans. In another connection, John's death comes as a relief to him, a chance to silence the voices crying out for help that he hears every day. Just as the lepers calling out to him for healing once overwhelmed Christ, so too is John exhausted by the weight of the world.

By seeing John as a Christ figure, readers are led to more carefully explore the book's theme of compassion. They

Argument Two
The author is moving on to the second part of her thesis. In the following paragraphs, she will prove: "By seeing John as a Christ figure, readers are led to more carefully explore the book's theme of compassion."

become aware of just how boundless John's selflessness is. He is on death row because of his compassion for the two little girls who had been violated and left for dead by William Wharton. When John tried to save their lives, he was caught and wrongly convicted of murdering them. John's compassion urges him to heal Paul's urinary tract infection without being asked. It also urges him to bring Mr. Jingles back to life for Eduard Delacroix's

Paul is increasingly drawn toward John as the story progresses.

sake and makes him willing to leave the prison to heal Melinda Moores.

As with Christ, John's compassion influences those around him. His compassion begins to be reflected in the other "good" characters of the novel. It leads the prison guards to accept Paul's plan for healing Melinda and attempt to make Delacroix's impending death easier by assuring him they will care for Mr. Jingles.

Argument Three

The author brings up her last point: "John's Christlike portrayal also heightens another important theme—sacrifice." After proving this argument in the next paragraphs, her thesis statement will be fully argued.

John's Christlike portrayal also heightens another important theme—sacrifice. Like Christ, John has been chosen to spend his life helping and healing—at a great personal cost. He has no home and no traditional family. He has sacrificed himself by attempting to help the two little girls. He stayed with their bodies after they were dead and did not try to run. His constant refrain, once he is found, is "I tried to take it back, but it was too late."[2] It is interpreted as an admission of guilt, but the phrase actually means John tried to erase what had happened to the girls—their rape and murder.

Heidi Strengell, author of *Dissecting Stephen King*, states, "[*The Green Mile*] discusses the existence of God, and . . . examines the possibility that Jesus Christ has returned repeatedly to our world over the centuries only to be crucified again and again."[3] Just as Christ willingly offered himself to the cross, John willingly offers himself to the green mile. In this way, John's execution is paralleled with Christ's crucifixion.

Through his sacrifice, John encounters Paul, Mr. Jingles, and other characters and takes their sins and illnesses upon himself. This is most vividly

Like Christ, John understands he must die.

represented by the tiny black bugs he exhales after a healing. The bugs symbolize sin and illness. When John holds in the bugs to pass onto Percy, John weakens. Even after releasing them, he remains weakened. It is as though he has kept part of humankind's sin and illness within himself. John is executed around middle age. He sacrifices years of life in order to heal others and provide them longer lives of their own.

Conclusion
This final paragraph is the conclusion of the critique. It sums up the author's arguments and partially restates the original thesis, which has now been argued and supported with evidence.

The Christlike character of John evokes the reader's collective unconscious knowledge of the archetypal Christ figure and elicits a powerful emotional response. Using this as a structure for understanding the book, the themes of compassion and sacrifice can be identified and examined. John Coffey embodies the novel's themes in a way readers can recognize in order to understand and connect with the book.

Thinking Critically about *The Green Mile*

Now it's your turn to assess the critique. Consider these questions:

1. The thesis argues that John Coffey's Christlike attributes allow readers to explore the book's themes of compassion and sacrifice. Do you agree with this thesis statement? Why or why not? Are there other themes you see in the novel? Could they be analyzed using an archetypal approach?

2. What was the most interesting argument made? What was the strongest one? What was the weakest? Were the points backed up with strong evidence from the book? Did the arguments support the thesis?

3. Do you think this conclusion does a good job of summarizing the main points in the novel and restating the thesis statement? Why or why not? How could it be better?

Other Approaches

The essay you read is one possible way to apply an archetypal approach to a critique of *The Green Mile*. What are some other ways you could approach it? Remember that analyzing a work using an archetypal approach will explore universal characters that have been represented in various forms for centuries.

Two alternate approaches follow. The first approach examines John as punishing rather than compassionate. The second links John's fate to Christ's as an innocent bound to die.

Flipping the Thesis Statement

Another essay might prove that John does not show compassion or sacrifice. When further explored, you may see that John actually judges and punishes the other characters in the book.

The thesis statement for such a critique might be: While John resembles a Christ figure, he does not embody a theme of compassion or sacrifice but rather embodies a theme of judgment. One point for this argument could be: John punishes Percy Wetmore by breathing the black bugs into Percy, which make him ill.

John's Predetermined Fate

Heidi Strengell, a critic of King's work, argues that John's fate is predetermined. His fate was set because of the circumstances of his birth—as an African American in the racist South. She also states his fate is predetermined because of his supernatural abilities, which are what make him a Christ figure. She states, "Coffey's supernatural healing ability and his race . . . isolate him from society and turn him into a freak in the eyes of his fellow human beings [and result in his destruction]. . . . Although the gift/curse molds his entire life, Coffey did nothing to deserve it."[4]

How could you use this information for a critique using an archetypal approach? The thesis statement might be: In *The Green Mile*, John's fate is predetermined because he is a Christ figure and because he is an African American in the racist South. One point could argue that Christ's fate was predetermined, too. Because John is a Christ figure, he was bound to die, even though he was innocent.

Essential Critiques

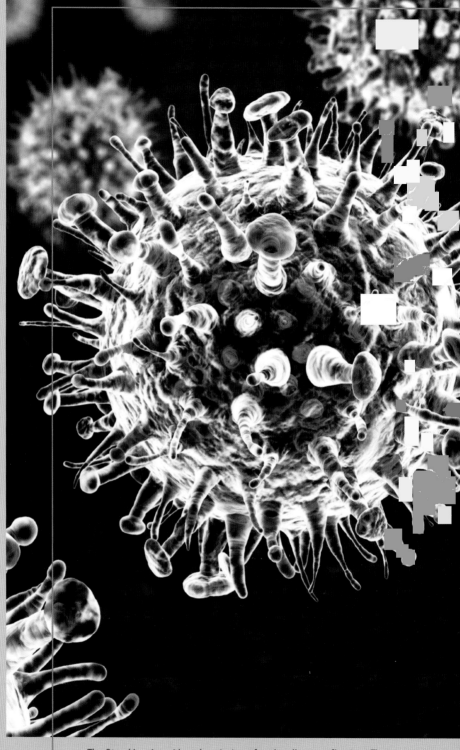

The Stand begins with a description of a deadly superflu virus. The infectious agent has spread across the United States and killed most of the population.

Summary of *The Stand*

King's novel *The Stand* was first published in 1978.
In 1990, King rereleased the book as *The Stand:
The Complete and Uncut Edition*. This version
contains revised material as well as sections that
were originally cut. It also changes the story's
setting from 1985 to 1990.

A Deadly Virus

The Stand is written in three sections. In the first
one, called "Captain Trips," a highly contagious and
deadly strain of superflu is accidentally released
from a government facility where it was being
developed as a biological weapon. Over the next 19
days, this superflu spreads around the world, killing
approximately 99 percent of the planet's population.
As the superflu kills more and more people, society

begins to break down. Readers are introduced to the few individuals who are resistant to the superflu. These survivors become the major characters of the novel, which follows their struggles to stay alive and protect their families and friends. These survivors include Fran Goldsmith, a college student from Maine; Stu Redman, a man from a small town in Texas; Larry Underwood, a rock star; and Nick Andros, who is both deaf and mute.

Dividing into Societies

In the second part of the book, "On the Border," survivors slowly divide into groups and make their way across the country. Some are united by the strange dreams of a 108-year-old woman named Mother Abagail who waits for them in Nebraska. A struggle between good and evil begins to unfold, with Mother Abagail as the symbol for goodness. When the groups of survivors reach Mother Abagail, she and the rest of the survivors move to Boulder, Colorado. The survivors establish the Boulder Free Zone and attempt to recreate a democratic government.

Other survivors gather in Las Vegas, Nevada. They are drawn to Randall Flagg, also known as the "Dark Man," who represents evil and possesses supernatural powers. This group of survivors establishes their own zone in Las Vegas that features a strong but harsh system of government. Flagg creates a weapons program with the idea of using it against the Free Zone followers. He sends one of his followers, Trashcan Man, out into the desert to search for weapons and bring them back to him.

At the Free Zone, Mother Abagail feels that she has sinned and become too proud of her leadership role. She goes off into the desert on a spiritual journey. Another member of the Free Zone, Harold Lauder, becomes increasingly bitter over his unrequited love for another survivor, Fran, from his hometown. She is pregnant with the child of her previous boyfriend, who died from the superflu. Harold Lauder and Nadine Cross, another Free Zone member who is secretly loyal to the Dark Man, set off a bomb at a Free Zone meeting. The explosion kills several people, including Nick Andros. Shortly after, Mother Abagail is found in an extremely weakened condition from her time in the desert. Before she dies, she asks four members of the Free Zone to travel to Las Vegas and confront Flagg. This becomes the "stand" of the novel's title and the third section of the book. In this section, good and evil confront each other.

Confrontation and an Open Ending

As the four men from the Free Zone travel toward Las Vegas, Stu Redman breaks his leg. He remains behind in Utah. The other three men reach Las Vegas, where they are imprisoned. One is tortured and executed by Flagg. The other two are put on display for public execution when Trashcan Man returns with a nuclear warhead. A giant, glowing hand called "the Hand of God" appears and detonates the warhead. It destroys Flagg, his followers, and the two remaining men from the Free Zone.

Back in Utah, Stu survives his injury and consequent illness. He weathers the Rocky Mountain winter with the help of Tom Cullen. Stu and Tom return to Boulder, where they find that Fran—who is now Stu's girlfriend—has had her baby. When the newborn baby develops the superflu, the survivors fear he will die, and humankind will end. But the baby recovers.

In the original version, the story ends with Stu asking Fran whether humankind will learn from

its mistakes. Fran replies she doesn't know. In the extended version, however, a final chapter had been added in which Randall Flagg, now known as Russell Faraday, awakens on a beach near a jungle and meets a group of native people. He begins to gather them as his new followers, saying, "Life was such a wheel that no man could stand upon it for long. And it always, in the end, came round to the same place again."[1] The line leaves the reader with a dark feeling that evil will begin again.

Mother Abagail symbolizes goodness in *The Stand*.

Economic problems in the United States during the 1970s, such as the gas shortage, may have influenced *The Stand*.

8

How to Apply Historical Criticism to *The Stand*

No. 2

What Is Historical Criticism?

Historical criticism explores a work of literature through the historical context in which it was written—not the time backdrop of the story itself. Many authors are influenced by national and international events that take place as they write. A reader may investigate how political, intellectual, and economic events of an era may have affected a work. Historical criticism involves not only reading the work itself but also researching the author's historical period.

Critique

During the 1970s, many Americans felt uneasy about the problems plaguing their country and the world. An oil shortage, high rates of inflation, and high unemployment rates forced people to live with less for the first time since World War II. New kinds of warfare, such as neutron bombs and chemical agents, were in development.

At the same time, Americans were losing faith in their government. Until 1975, the Vietnam War had dragged on despite popular opinion against it. In 1974, the nation had faced a different kind of disgrace. Facing almost certain impeachment, President Richard Nixon resigned from office as a result of the Watergate scandal—he had been involved in illegal actions to win reelection in 1972. As King said:

> Writing [the book The Stand] came during a troubled time for the world in general and America in particular; we were suffering from our first gas [shortage] in history, we had just witnessed the sorry end of the Nixon administration and the first presidential resignation in history, we had been resoundingly defeated in [the Vietnam War], and we were grappling with a host of domestic problems.[1]

The Watergate scandal and President Nixon's resignation contributed to the suspicion of government many Americans felt during the 1970s.

Although King revised and updated *The Stand* in the late 1980s, he originally wrote it in the United States during the late 1970s. The novel was deeply influenced by this historical era. *The Stand* reflects and explores the fears of many Americans regarding the government and warfare during the late 1970s.

Thesis Statement

The thesis statement in this critique is: "*The Stand* reflects and explores the fears of many Americans regarding the government and warfare during the late 1970s." This thesis addresses the question: How was *The Stand* influenced by the period in which it was written?

Argument One

The author has started the argument to support her thesis. Her first point is: "The basic plot of *The Stand* reflects lack of faith in and suspicion of government." The introduction of the critique details these same feelings in Americans during the time *The Stand* was written. This point draws the parallel between the historical period and the book.

The basic plot of *The Stand* reflects lack of faith in and suspicion of government. A government laboratory makes a superflu germ for biological warfare that is accidentally released and destroys humanity. One line in particular points to the government's conspiring ways: "Somebody made a mistake . . . and they're trying to cover it up."[2]

Not only is the government responsible for the release of the superflu, but it also uses violence to suppress the results of the epidemic. Rioting students on a college campus are slaughtered by government troops. This closely echoes the notorious day in 1970 at Kent State University in Ohio, when students protesting the Vietnam War were killed by National Guard troops. In King's novel, though, the evil goes much deeper: Soldiers then kill members of the media reporting on the event.

The Stand also reflects another deep cultural fear of the 1970s—that of chemical and biological weapons. People were beginning to learn about chemical weapons, including VX nerve gas, Agent Orange defoliant, ricin, and sarin. Even though President Nixon had declared a moratorium on the development of new chemical warfare agents, the existing agents were not banned. King has said that he got the idea for *The Stand* after an incident in Utah in 1968. There, a canister of nerve gas spilled, supposedly on its way to a disposal facility, and its contents killed thousands of sheep. The news report stated that if the wind had been blowing in the opposite direction, the same substance could have affected the people of Salt Lake City, Utah. In *The Stand,* King shows just how difficult it is for the government to control deadly agents. As Stu Redman says, "My guess is that . . . there was an accident someplace. Like what happened to those sheep in Utah thirty years ago, only a lot worse."[3] Even though it created the superflu, the government in *The Stand* cannot successfully cure it, and the controls it had in place to safeguard society fail.

> **Argument Two**
> The author's second point is: "*The Stand* also reflects another deep cultural fear of the 1970s—that of chemical and biological weapons." In this point, the author again draws the parallels between the historical period and the novel.

In the 1970s, Americans were also worried about the threat of nuclear destruction due to the Cold War. Despite arms talks, both the United States and the Soviet Union were developing new nuclear missiles. Each had enough weapons to destroy every city in the world. Many people questioned if humankind could comprehend the consequences of this amazing power that technology had wrought. The plot of *The Stand* demonstrates the fear and skepticism many Americans felt about nuclear weapons. One of Randall Flagg's initial actions in creating his zone in Las Vegas is to send Trashcan Man out into the desert. Trashcan Man, who is mentally unstable and already prone to destruction, is to locate military weapons stockpiles and missile silos with nuclear weapons that could be used against the members of the Boulder Free Zone. Trashcan Man does deliver a nuclear weapon to Flagg, who either does not understand or care that it could harm the group. The bomb's detonation results in the destruction of Flagg and his followers.

Argument Three

The final point the author makes is: "The plot of *The Stand* demonstrates the fear and skepticism many Americans felt about nuclear weapons." This argument connects an aspect of the book, nuclear weapons, to the historical time period in which *The Stand* was written.

The threat of nuclear warfare during the 1970s was reflected in *The Stand*.

Through Flagg, King shows how technology provides opportunities for those who are inept or without conscience. King shows one of Americans' greatest fears of the time—what would happen if weapons of mass destruction fell into the hands of a terrorist. As literary critic Heidi Strengell put it, "In other words, not only is humanity's existence threatened by national weaponry systems but, worse still, by the whims of maniacs who would eagerly push the red button."[4]

> **Conclusion**
>
> This final paragraph is the conclusion of the critique. It sums up the author's arguments and partially restates the original thesis, which has now been argued and supported with historical and textual evidence.

During the 1970s, many Americans moved away from the prosperity and hope of the 1950s and 1960s into a time of distrust and disillusionment with their government and a fear of nuclear warfare and chemical and biological weapons. Americans began to question their government's actions and whether they could feel safe in the midst of new methods of warfare. In a direct correlation to the time period in which it was written, *The Stand* represents the same fears and asks the same questions.

Thinking Critically about *The Stand*

Now it's your turn to assess the critique.
Consider these questions:

1. The thesis argues that *The Stand*'s plot and tone
   were directly affected by the events and social
   attitudes of the time period in which it was
   written. Do you agree with this thesis statement?
   Why or why not?

2. What was the most interesting argument made?
   What was the strongest one? What was the
   weakest? Were the points backed up with strong
   evidence from the book? Did the arguments
   support the thesis?

3. Can you find other textual evidence from the
   summary that would contribute to the thesis?
   Are you aware of any other historical evidence
   that would contribute to the essay?

Other Approaches

The previous critique is just one way to apply a historical criticism to *The Stand*. What are some other ways? Remember that the goal is to determine how or whether a work has been influenced by current events or social attitudes at the time it was written. Following are two alternate approaches. The first examines how historical events may have impacted the revised ending of the novel in 1990. The second approach discusses another way skepticism of government is portrayed.

Revised Ending

In *Stephen King: A Critical Companion*, Sharon A. Russell comments on King's expanded version of *The Stand*: "Some critics feel that, in addition to adding information about the characters and detailing the course of the superflu, which sets the plot in motion, King shifts the tone of the novel in the [newer] complete version."[5] Do you feel that the added ending shifts the tone of the book? How? How might the wars, debt crisis, and political strife of the 1980s account for King's revisions?

Such questions may lead you to this thesis statement: The revised version of *The Stand* reflects U.S. cultural changes from 1978 to 1990. Instead of showing fear of war and distrust of government, this new edition offers a bleak cynical approach to the state of the world.

Skepticism of Government

Another approach focuses on skepticism of government and its consequences. Many survivors of the superflu are those who did not blindly accept what the government told them about the illness or what they should do. For example, Stu Redman actively fought against the government officials who held him in a medical facility. Many characters who did what they were told or allowed themselves to be taken to government medical facilities did not survive.

The thesis statement for a critique that specifically examines the novel's skepticism of government may be: In *The Stand*, skepticism of government, which many Americans felt during the late 1970s, is one of the main tools of survival during the superflu pandemic.

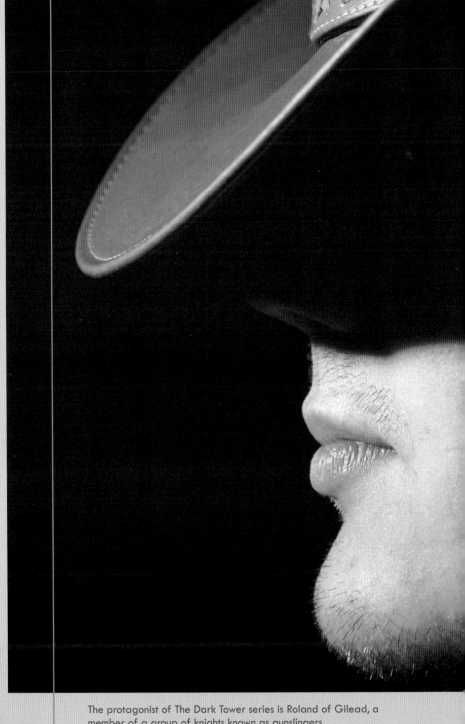

The protagonist of The Dark Tower series is Roland of Gilead, a member of a group of knights known as gunslingers.

Summary of The Dark Tower Series

The Dark Tower series, which was published over a period of 22 years, comprises seven separate books: *The Gunslinger* (1982), *The Drawing of the Three* (1987), *The Waste Lands* (1991), *Wizard and Glass* (1997), *Wolves of the Calla* (2003), *Song of Susannah* (2004), and *The Dark Tower* (2004). King has called this work his magnum opus, the chief work of his entire career.

A Mixed-Genre Series

The Dark Tower series is not strictly written in the horror genre, as are many of King's works. The series incorporates themes from many different types of writing, including fantasy, science fiction, horror, and Westerns. King said of the work, "I had recently seen a bigger-than-life Sergio Leone

Western, and it had me wondering what would happen if you brought two very distinct genres together: heroic fantasy and the Western."[1]

King began writing The Dark Tower series when he was 19 years old. He readily admits that he started it at a time when J. R. R. Tolkien's *The Lord of the Rings* saga was popular. However, he wanted his quest to take place in a Western setting.

The Main Character

The story in all seven books revolves around Roland of Gilead, the last living member of a group of knights known as gunslingers. The story takes place in a parallel universe—a fantasy world similar to but not exactly like Earth. Like the Wild West, this world is primitive and stark. However, remnants of a long-lost magical realm and a highly technological society still exist. Roland's world is on the edge of destruction. Many formerly powerful nations have been torn apart by war, and entire cities and regions have vanished without a trace. Here, time does not flow in a normal, chronological fashion.

Roland is on a quest to find the Dark Tower, a building fabled to be the center of all the universes.

Roland believes that by reaching the Dark Tower, he will save humanity from destruction, which justifies the loss of many of the companions he meets along the way. These many characters will become either friends or enemies, and all are bound by a sense of destiny or fate called "ka."

Much of the setting of The Dark Tower series is a dilapidated and torn-apart world.

Book One: *The Gunslinger*

In *The Gunslinger*, Roland makes his way across the desert in his quest for the Dark Tower. He meets several characters. In one encounter, Roland tells about his past and how he had to kill every resident of a town called Tull in order to escape the town alive. At a way station, Roland, who is near death from walking through the desert, meets a character called Jake, who died in his own parallel universe. Jake nurses Roland back to health. Together, Roland and Jake travel out of the desert and toward a mountain. Roland's greatest enemy in book one, the Man in Black, appears. He forces Roland to choose between his own life and Jake's. Jake falls to his death, and Roland falls asleep.

Book Two: *The Drawing of the Three*

In *The Drawing of the Three*, Roland awakens. In a confrontation with a group of lobsterlike creatures, he loses several fingers, a toe, and a portion of his leg. Weak and feverish from infection, he struggles to continue traveling on his path. Roland finds three doors and enters each of them one at a time. They lead to New York City during three different time periods. Roland is put in contact with three characters: Odetta (whose multiple personalities will fuse into one identity known as Susannah), Eddie, and an evil character named Mort the Pusher. Roland learns about these characters from their own points of view and ultimately saves Susannah and Eddie in different ways. They continue on Roland's quest with him, although he realizes that he may have to sacrifice them before he gets to the Dark Tower.

Book Three: *The Waste Lands*

The Waste Lands continues with Roland and his two companions traveling to a place called Mid-World, the name given to Roland's version of Earth. The group encounters two characters who join Roland's gang: Jake from *The Gunslinger*, who has returned from the dead, and a strange creature named Oy, a combination of a badger and a raccoon. Their path leads them to a nearly destroyed city called Lud, where Jake is kidnapped. However, he is later reunited with the others. Known as the ka-tet, the group boards a computerized train that carries them across the wastelands. This lifeless area has been decimated by a disaster said to have been worse than a nuclear war.

Book Four: *Wizard and Glass*

In *Wizard and Glass*, the members of Roland's group leave the train in Topeka, Kansas. Here it is the 1980s, and the city has been abandoned because of the same flu that King wrote about in *The Stand*. As the ka-tet camps there, Roland tells them about how he earned his guns and came of age. The following day, the ka-tet reaches the Emerald City, one of several allusions to *The Wizard of Oz*. Roland confronts Randall Flagg, a character from *The Stand*. Roland tries to shoot Flagg but misses, and Flagg disappears. The group moves on. Eddie, Susannah, and Jake refuse to separate from Roland, even though they have learned from his past that most of his companions do not survive.

Book Five: *Wolves of the Calla*

In *Wolves of the Calla*, the ka-tet travels to a farm village where they meet the townspeople, one of whom is Father Callahan from King's novel *'Salem's Lot*. The townspeople need help defending themselves against a group of wolves that appear once every generation and steal children. At the same time, Roland and his ka-tet have to protect a single red rose, which is growing in Manhattan in the year 1977. If the rose is destroyed, the Dark Tower will fall. Susannah has begun to show strange behavior, and it is revealed that she is possessed by a demon. She is also pregnant with

Roland's child. At the end of the book, Roland's group succeeds in defeating the wolves. Another personality within Susannah, Mia, takes over her body and uses a magic object to transport herself to Manhattan.

In several parts of the series, Roland must trek across a barren desert to reach his destination.

Book Six: *Song of Susannah*

Song of Susannah takes place largely in realistic Manhattan, where the group has gone to find Susannah. Controlled by Mia, Susannah knows she will give birth to a son named Mordred. The ka-tet must find Susannah and gain possession of the vacant lot where the rose grows. In this book, Roland and Eddie find themselves near King's home in Maine. King, as the author, plays a role in the story. His character dies on June 19, 1999—the date of the author's nearly fatal car accident. The book ends with Jake and Father Callahan about to enter a New York City vampire diner, where they hope to find Susannah.

Book Seven: *The Dark Tower*

In the final volume, *The Dark Tower*, Susannah gives birth to Mordred, who is not only Roland's son but also the son of an evil character called the Crimson King. Mordred can shape-shift. He attempts to eat his mother right after birth, but she shoots and wounds him. Roland and his group jump back in time to save Stephen King from death, since they believe they will succeed only if he survives to write about them. Mordred, who hates Roland, finally reaches him and attacks him. However, Oy defends Roland, which buys enough time for Roland to kill Mordred. The book and the series end with Roland finding and entering the Dark Tower. Once inside it, he finds a door marked with his name. Roland realizes he has reached the Dark

Tower many times before and will continue to do
so until he understands that the Dark Tower is not
the center of all the universes. He is then teleported
back to the desert, with no memory of his quest,
to begin all over again. This time, however, he
has been given an object, the Horn of Eld, which
may help him finally succeed in the quest. The
series ends with the same sentence it began with:
"The man in black fled across the desert, and the
gunslinger followed."[2]

The structure of a hero quest extends back to Homer's epic poem titled *The Odyssey* and tales of knights.

10

How to Apply Structuralist Criticism to The Dark Tower Series

What Is Structuralist Criticism?

Structuralism is a system of criticism that looks at the underlying, unchanging patterns that works of literature have in common. These patterns can include plots, themes, and characters. Critics of this school of theory use these patterns to find meaning in a work.

One of the ways structuralist criticism can be applied to a work of fiction is by looking at common myths and types of literature found across many different cultures and time periods. These types of literature include comedy, romance, tragedy, satire, and the hero's quest. By looking at the common elements, or structures, within a certain type of literature, the reader can then make a comparison: How does the work at hand compare

to the defining elements of its genre? What are
its patterns, and how do they fit together with
patterns in other similar works? The reader can then
comment on how the work fits within the tradition
of its structure and how that tradition has persisted
through history.

Critique

One of the oldest types of literature is the hero
quest, which has been told for thousands of years
and across many cultures, from the ancient Greek
story of *The Odyssey* to stories of King Arthur. It
is rooted in classic books such as *The Lord of the
Rings* and contemporary books such as the Harry
Potter series.

The hero quest exhibits a set of specific
characteristics, regardless of its exact plot and
characters. The quest itself often entails a literal
journey across a physical distance as well as a
symbolic or emotional journey that changes the
hero character. Born under unusual circumstances,
the hero usually is in danger. He or she is often
a member of royalty who leaves home and lives
with others. Generally, an event leads the hero on a
quest. Often, a special weapon that only he or she

can use is present. The hero usually has supernatural help and must pass many tests of character during the journey. As the journey continues, the hero may have wounds that cannot be healed. The hero may also be granted forgiveness from family members. Upon death, the hero is usually rewarded with spiritual enlightenment.

According to Vladimir Propp in *Morphology of the Folktale*, hero quests in ancient mythology have even more specific criteria. The main character violates some sort of rule that results in banishment or a task to fulfill. There is an encounter with a villain, a magical or supernatural creature, and three different creatures, who either help or are helped by the hero. The hero is tested and must battle the forces of evil, which are vanquished using the hero's special gifts. The hero survives and gains knowledge, a marriage, or money. By using the structure of a hero quest, The Dark Tower exhibits a main theme in the series: the journey is more important than the final destination.

Thesis Statement

The thesis statement in this critique is: "By using the structure of a hero quest, The Dark Tower exhibits a main theme in the series: the journey is more important than the final destination." This thesis addresses the questions: What is the overarching structure in The Dark Tower series, and how does this structure contribute to the meaning of the text?

Roland of Gilead is a hero figure. He displays most of the attributes given to a main character in a hero quest. The story hints that he may be a king or of royal blood, and his family's destiny is to pursue the Dark Tower. As with a knight of medieval times, he has been trained to use weapons in his father's castle. On his quest to reach the Dark Tower, he brings the gun he has earned and only he can use.

Roland receives supernatural help at many points in his journey. He also receives a wound that will not heal: the loss of his fingers on his gun hand. A group of close friends assist him and he helps them—as is the case with Frodo Baggins of *The Lord of the Rings* and Harry Potter. Roland also survives several tests, both physical and mental. Although he is not perfect, his companions trust him as their leader.

Roland's story would also fit with Propp's more specific criteria for a mythological hero quest. The reader learns that Roland has taken an early test of

Roland has been trained to fight in battle, but instead of using a sword, he uses a gun.

his manhood and alienates his family, forcing him into his quest for the Dark Tower. He encounters an oracle trapped in an enchanted circle of stone. He is then guided by creatures who provide him with information. He is tested when he must leave behind a young boy who is like a son to him. Roland then uses his knowledge and his companions' help to beat the Man in Black. Roland survives to gain wisdom.

Argument Two

The author's second point begins illustrating the importance of Roland's journey: "Throughout his journey, Roland learns several important lessons that teach him about the meaning of his existence."

Throughout his journey, Roland learns several important lessons that teach him about the meaning of his existence. Roland learns to love again. He had renounced the emotion because he believed it brought heartache and suffering. Unable to stop the murder of Susan Delgado, his true love, Roland had blamed himself. Growing up, he also saw the failure of his parents' marriage after his mother committed adultery. However, by the end of his quest, as he is about to reach the Dark Tower, he has fallen in love with Susannah. Roland also learns about mercy. Previously, he would have gunned down the people who had wronged him.

By the end, however, Roland is willing to be merciful to Mordred—who had tried to kill him. Roland promises to free Mordred in exchange for Roland's companion Oy.

Argument Three

The author's final point is: "The fact that there is no definitive end to Roland's quest is a major clue that the journey is what is most important in The Dark Tower." The next paragraphs detail the importance of seemingly endless hero quests.

The fact that there is no definitive end to Roland's quest is a major clue that the journey is what is most important in The Dark Tower. When Roland finally reaches the Dark Tower, he realizes that he must continue to relive the quest until he accomplishes what he is intended to achieve. The endless quest is also a feature of the King Arthur legends and J. R. R. Tolkien's *The Lord of the Rings*. In the Arthurian legends, once Arthur dies, he moves to Avalon, where he will someday awaken again when he is needed. Frodo of *The Lord of the Rings* travels to the Valinor at the end of his life, a place where immortal beings live.

Roland believes that reaching the Dark Tower will save humankind from destruction, thereby justifying the sacrifice of his friends along the way, including Jake. However, once he gets there, he realizes he will repeat his journey, continuing his quest over and over again until he gains enough knowledge to end the cycle. What Roland must come to understand is that the real keys to his quest are the wisdom he gains and the relationships he builds. Roland will hopefully one day realize that he does not have to reach the Dark Tower. Instead, he can focus on the people around him and his own world, abandoning the quest. As Bev Vincent writes in *The Road to the Dark Tower*, "It may take him several more tries, but King leaves hope that eventually Roland will find what he seeks—his own humanity and the meaning of his existence—at the end of the road to the Dark Tower."[1]

Conclusion

This final paragraph is the conclusion of the critique. It sums up the author's arguments and partially restates the original thesis, which has now been argued and supported with evidence.

Looking at The Dark Tower series through the structure of the hero quest allows for an exploration of the larger theme—above and beyond what is taking place in the plot. As with most hero quests, Roland's journey is more important than his final destination. As King put it, "I hope you came to hear the tale, and not the ending. For an ending, you only have to turn to the last page and see what is there writ upon. But endings are heartless. An ending is a closed door no man . . . can open."[2]

Thinking Critically about The Dark Tower

Now it's your turn to assess the critique.
Consider these questions:

1. The thesis argues that the hero quest structure in The Dark Tower series infuses meaning in the books. Do you agree with this thesis statement? Why or why not?

2. What was the most interesting argument made? What was the strongest one? What was the weakest? Were the points backed up with strong evidence from the book? Did the arguments support the thesis?

3. Does this critique effectively summarize the author's arguments? How else could the author have ended this critique?

Other Approaches

The critique you read is one possible way to apply a structuralist approach to The Dark Tower series. What are some other ways? Remember that structuralist critiques examine underlying elements as a way of understanding a work. Following are two alternate approaches. The first makes a new argument using the idea of a journey. The second examines the series as part of the Western genre.

Not about the Journey

The Dark Tower series may be a hero quest, but does this structure have to show the importance of a journey? Not necessarily. An alternate thesis focusing on the hero quest could be: The never-ending journey of the hero quest as seen in The Dark Tower series demonstrates a lack of meaning within the novels. To support this point, one might show that Roland continually retraces his steps, without knowing he is doing so. He is unable to learn from his mistakes, therefore making the journey an endless, pointless process.

Viewed as Western Novels

The hero quest is not the only structuralist element that can be taken from The Dark Tower series. Because the series contains elements of several other literary genres, there are additional patterns to examine. For example, the series has a strong Western component: Roland is a gunslinger, he rides a horse, the terrain often seems like the Wild West, and the language is reminiscent of Western novels. How do the Western elements in The Dark Tower series contribute to meaning in the novels? The thesis statement that addresses this question might be: The Western elements found throughout The Dark Tower series demonstrate that Roland is governed not by societal rules but by his own moral code.

You Critique It

Now that you have learned about different critical theories and how to apply them to literature, are you ready to perform your own critique? You have read that this type of evaluation can help you look at literature in a new way and make you pay attention to certain issues you may not have otherwise recognized. So, why not use one of the critical theories profiled in this book to consider a fresh take on your favorite book?

First, choose a theory and the book you want to analyze. Remember that the theory is a springboard for asking questions about the work.

Next, write a specific question that relates to the theory you have selected. Then you can form your thesis, which should provide the answer to that question. Your thesis is the most important part of your critique and offers an argument about the work based on the tenets, or beliefs, of the theory you are applying. Recall that the thesis statement typically appears at the very end of the introductory paragraph of your essay. It is usually only one sentence long.

After you have written your thesis, find evidence to back it up. Good places to start are in the work itself or in journals or articles that discuss what other people have said about it. Since you are critiquing a book, you may also want to read about the author's life so you can get a sense of what factors may have affected the creative process. This can be especially useful if working within historical, biographical, or psychological criticism.

Depending on which theory you are applying, you can often find evidence in the book's language, plot, or character development. You should also explore parts of the book that seem to disprove your thesis and create an argument against them. As you do this, you might want to address what other critics have written about the book. Their quotes may help support your claim.

Before you start analyzing a work, think about the different arguments made in this book. Reflect on how evidence supporting the thesis was presented. Did you find that some of the techniques used to back up the arguments were more convincing than others? Try these methods as you prove your thesis in your own critique.

When you are finished writing your critique, read it over carefully. Is your thesis statement understandable? Do the supporting arguments flow logically, with the topic of each paragraph clearly stated? Can you add any information that would present your readers with a stronger argument in favor of your thesis? Were you able to use quotes from the book, as well as from other critics, to enhance your ideas?

Did you see the work in a new light?

Timeline

1965 King publishes his first short story, "I Was a Teenage Grave Robber."

1966 King enrolls in the University of Maine at Orono.

1947 Stephen King is born on September 21 in Portland, Maine.

1987 The second book of The Dark Tower series, *The Drawing of the Three*, is published.

1996 *The Green Mile* is published as a serial in six installments; later it is published in one volume.

King receives the O. Henry Award for Best American Short Story for "The Man in the Black Suit."

1990 *The Stand* is republished in a revised and uncut edition.

1991 The third book of The Dark Tower series, *The Waste Lands*, is published.

1997 The fourth book of The Dark Tower series, *Wizard and Glass*, is published.

1999 On June 19, King is struck by a car and badly injured.

1967
King's first short story in his professional career, "The Glass Floor," is published.

1970
King graduates with a Bachelor of Arts degree in English.

1971
King marries Tabitha Spruce in January.

1974
King's first novel, *Carrie*, is published.

1978
The Stand is published.

King begins teaching creative writing at the University of Maine.

1982
The first book of The Dark Tower series, *The Gunslinger*, is published.

2002
King announces that he will retire from writing; however, he continues to write and to publish.

King receives the Lifetime Achievement Award by the Horror Writer's Association.

2003
The fifth book of The Dark Tower series, *Wolves of the Calla*, is published.

King is awarded a Medal for Distinguished Contribution to American Letters by the National Book Foundation.

2004
The sixth book of The Dark Tower series, *Song of Susannah*, is published.

The final book in The Dark Tower series, *The Dark Tower*, is published.

2007
King receives a Lifetime Achievement Award from the Canadian Literary Guild.

2009
King announces that he will begin contributing to a new comic book series called American Vampire.

Glossary

archetype
>A model of behavior or personality that can be identified in works of literature.

collective unconscious
>The part of the mind that includes a vast array of human experiences as a species.

genre
>A class or category of written work, such as horror, science fiction, and fantasy.

magnum opus
>A great work; usually the chief work of a writer's career.

misogynistic
>Showing a hatred of women.

patriarchal
>Ruled by men.

personal conscious
>The part of the mind that is in a wakened state.

personal unconscious
>The part of the mind that contains memories.

philanthropist
>A person who donates money, property, or time to help the poor or for human welfare and advancement.

protagonist
>The main character in a fictional work.

serial
> A story published in short installments at regular intervals.

telekinesis
> The ability to move objects with the mind.

tenet
> A belief generally held to be true.

theme
> A subject or an idea that occurs throughout an artistic work.

Bibliography of Works and Criticism

Important Works

Carrie, 1974

'Salem's Lot, 1974

The Shining, 1976

The Stand, 1978

The Dead Zone, 1979

Cujo, 1981

Danse Macabre, 1981

The Dark Tower I: The Gunslinger, 1982

Pet Sematary, 1982

It, 1986

The Tommyknockers, 1986

Misery, 1987

The Dark Tower II: The Drawing of the Three, 1987

The Stand: The Complete & Uncut Edition, 1990

Needful Things, 1990

The Dark Tower III: The Waste Lands, 1991

Dolores Claiborne, 1992

Nightmares & Dreamscapes, 1993

Desperation, 1995

The Green Mile, 1996

The Dark Tower IV: Wizard and Glass, 1997

Storm of the Century, 1999

The Girl Who Loved Tom Gordon, 1999

On Writing: A Memoir of the Craft, 1999

Riding the Bullet, 2000

Dreamcatcher, 2000

The Dark Tower V: Wolves of the Calla, 2003

The Dark Tower VI: Song of Susannah, 2004

The Dark Tower VII: The Dark Tower, 2004

Cell, 2006

Duma Key, 2008

Just After Sunset, 2008

Under the Dome, 2009

Blockade Billy, 2010

Critical Discussions

Magistrale, Tony. *Landscape of Fear: Stephen King's American Gothic*. Bowling Green, OH: Bowling Green State University Press, 1988.

Russell, Sharon A. *Stephen King: A Critical Companion*. Westport, CT: Greenwood Press, 1996.

Strengell, Heidi. *Dissecting Stephen King: From the Gothic to Literary Naturalism*. Madison, WI: University of Wisconsin Press, 2005.

Vincent, Bev. *The Road to the Dark Tower: Exploring Stephen King's Magnum Opus*. New York: New American Library, 2004.

Resources

Selected Bibliography

King, Stephen. *Carrie: Collector's Edition*. New York: New American Library, 1991.

King, Stephen. *The Green Mile: The Complete Serial Novel*. New York: Pocket Books, 1996.

King, Stephen. *The Gunslinger*. New York: Signet Books, 2003.

King, Stephen. *Stephen King's Danse Macabre*. New York: Berkeley Books, 1981.

Further Readings

Collings, Michael A. *The Many Facets of Stephen King*. San Bernandino, CA: Borgo Press, 2008.

Gresh, Lois H., and Robert Weinberg. *The Science of Stephen King: From Carrie to Cell, The Terrifying Truth Behind the Horror Master's Fiction*. Hoboken, NJ: John Wiley, 2007.

King, Stephen. *The Drawing of the Three*. New York: Signet Books, 2003.

King, Stephen. *The Stand: Complete and Uncut Edition*. New York: Doubleday, 1990.

Web Links

To learn more about critiquing the works of Stephen King, visit ABDO Publishing Company online at **www.abdopublishing.com**. Web sites about the works of Stephen King are featured on our Book Links page. These links are routinely monitored and updated to provide the most current information available.

For More Information

Horror Writers Association

244 5th Avenue, Suite 2767, New York, NY 10001

www.horror.org

The Horror Writers Association, of which Stephen King is a member, is a resource for authors who write in the horror genre. The organization presents awards to horror authors, gives writing and market tips, and includes news releases on newly released horror fiction.

StephenKing.com

www.stephenking.com/index.html

In addition to having a biography and photo gallery of the author, Stephen King's official Web site includes information on King's complete list of works, author appearances, and other news.

Source Notes

Chapter 1. Introduction to Critiques
None.

Chapter 2. A Closer Look at Stephen King
1. "Stephen King: Recipient of the National Book Foundation 2003 Medal for Distinguished Contribution to American Letters." National Book Foundation. 15 Sept. 2003. 2 Feb. 2010 <http://www.nationalbook.org/dcal_2003.html>.

Chapter 3. Summary of *Carrie*
None.

Chapter 4. How to Apply Feminist Criticism to *Carrie*
1. Eph. 5:22–23. *Holy Bible, New Living Translation*. Wheaton, IL: Tyndale House Publishers, 2004.

2. Stephen King. *Carrie (Collector's Edition)*. New York: Penguin, 1981. 24–25.

3. Ibid. 32.

4. Ibid. 76.

5. Ibid. 59.

6. Ibid. 73.

7. Kate Cielinski. "Pig's Blood for a Pig." *How to Build a Better Monster*. 31 Oct. 2004. 18 Feb. 2010 <http://blogs.setonhill.edu/KateCielinski/005573.html>.

8. Ibid.

Chapter 5. Summary of *The Green Mile*

None.

Chapter 6. How to Apply Archetype Theory to *The Green Mile*

1. Stephen King. *The Green Mile*. New York: Scribner, 2000. 20.

2. Ibid. 315.

3. Heidi Strengell. *Dissecting Stephen King: From the Gothic to Literary Naturalism*. Madison, WI: University of Wisconsin Press, 2005. 211.

4. Ibid. 212.

Chapter 7. Summary of *The Stand*

1. Stephen King. *The Stand: The Complete & Uncut Edition*. New York: Doubleday, 1990. 1153.

Chapter 8. How to Apply Historical Criticism to *The Stand*

1. Stephen King. *Danse Macabre*. New York: Berkley Books, 1981. 400.

2. Stephen King. *The Stand: The Complete & Uncut Edition*. New York: Doubleday, 1990. 152.

3. Ibid. 108.

Source Notes Continued

4. Heidi Strengell. *Dissecting Stephen King: From the Gothic to Literary Naturalism.* Madison, WI: University of Wisconsin Press, 2005. 145.

5. Sharon A. Russell. *Stephen King: A Critical Companion.* Westport, CT: Greenwood Press, 1996. 64.

Chapter 9. Summary of The Dark Tower Series

1. Bev Vincent. *The Road to the Dark Tower: Exploring Stephen King's Magnum Opus.* New York: New American Library, 2004. 8.

2. Stephen King. *The Dark Tower.* New York: Scribner, 2004. 830.

Chapter 10. How to Apply Structuralist Criticism to The Dark Tower Series

1. Bev Vincent. *The Road to the Dark Tower: Exploring Stephen King's Magnum Opus.* New York: New American Library, 2004. 191.

2. Ibid. 276.

About the Author

Marcia Amidon Lusted is the author of more than 40 books
and more than 100 magazine articles, all for young readers.
She is also an assistant editor for Cobblestone Publishing, as
well as a writing instructor and musician. She lives in New
Hampshire.

Photo Credits

Gregg DeGuire/WireImage/Getty Images, cover (foreground),
3; Stefan Klein/iStockphoto, cover (left), 27, 45, 63, 85;
Christian Delbert/iStockphoto, back cover, 13, 19, 39, 57, 75;
David Newton/iStockphoto, cover (right), 7; Peter Kramer/
AP Images, 12, 98 (top); Aaron Harris/AP Images, 17, 99;
United Artists/Photofest, 18, 21, 24, 26, 33; Warner Brothers/
Photofest, 38, 43, 44, 49, 51; Björn Meyer/iStockphoto, 56;
ABC/Photofest, 61; AP Images, 62, 69; NBC Newswire/AP
Images, 65; Valeria Titova/iStockphoto, 74; iStockphoto, 77;
Tobias Helbig/iStockphoto, 81, 98 (bottom); Vladimir Nikulin/
iStockphoto, 84; Roberto A Sanchez/iStockphoto, 89